THE STEN COOKBOOK

By Allan Cole

From The Novel Series
by Allan Cole & Chris Bunch

For Kathryn
Who Suggested This Book
And Did Much Of The Work

To Chris
My Late Partner In Crime

And To Sean Moon
Who Started The Whole Clottin' Thing…

The Sten Cookbook:
A Foreword

Actually, this ought to be called "The Eternal Emperor's Cookbook," because that's who started the whole business. A gourmet from way, way back, the Eternal Emperor cooked up at least one dish for nearly every episode of Sten. When he stopped cooking, of course, is when the drakh hit the clottin' fan.

My late partner, Chris Bunch, and I made cooking an integral part of the Emperor's character to help humanize him. This was a guy, after all, who over several thousand years had leveraged his discovery and control of the ultimate source of energy into a Galactic Empire with billions upon billions of subjects - both alien and human alike. (Although the word "alien" was considered bigoted in Sten's world and the term "Beings" was preferred.)

We didn't want some brooding despot of a monarch, who slouched on an enormous throne dispensing injustice and misery right and left just for the clot of it. We wanted the Emperor down to earth - making that quality as much a part of his success as the secret of immortality and Anti-Matter Two. (AM2)

Chris and I built in a longing for the good old days of the Twenty Second Century. The Emperor is constantly tinkering in his workshops, trying to duplicate everything from the best formula for varnish used on really good acoustic guitars to his beloved Scotch, which he misses most of all.

He's also constantly trying to recreate the dishes of his youth, spending fortunes - both large and small - to bring crucial herbs and spices back from extinction.

The Emperor, we decided, would be a man who started life at the very bottom rung. Born to a family who owned a small diner on the polluted - and overcrowded - main island of Hawaii, he's orphaned at an early age but still has vivid memories of family members working and laughing in the diner's kitchen. His father liked to boast that he could not only duplicate any dish but improve upon the recipe. The scent and taste of those marvelous creations haunt his dreams for many hundreds of years.

Allan Cole

The main rule Chris and I imposed on the books was that the recipes had to have something to do with the book's plot, or the scene in which the cooking occurs.

If the Emp is considering dropping a planet buster on an enemy, for example, Nuked Hen becomes the Dish Du Jour. A night spent pondering diplomatic twists and turns over several jugs of Scotch - then bring on Angelo Stew, the ultimate hangover cure.

In Sten #3 - The Court Of A Thousand Suns - we added Marr and Senn, Imperial caterers who provided us with more interesting recipes, also conjured up by the Milchian pair to fit the theme of the occasion.

Finally, as time went by we let Sten and his sidekick - Alex Kilgour - offer up a few dishes. Mainly because near the end the Emperor loses his cooking mojo and the stories take a nastier turn.

The idea for the cookbook was inspired some years ago by a young Coast Guard lieutenant who was an avid reader of Sten. In an e-mail he said that while at sea he always took his turn cooking dinner, even though he was the captain of the vessel.

Allan Cole

He particularly loved cooking the dishes in the Sten novels. He said, "The new guys must have thought the old man mad, to see him hovering over the galley, big spoon in one hand, a greasy science fiction book in the other."

(Side note: A science fiction version of that scene was recreated in The Hate Parallax, a novel I wrote with Russian author Nick Perumov. Check it out here: http://tinyurl.com/3qr7qpc)

My wife, Kathryn, had been after us for a long time to put together a Sten cookbook. The e-mail was the tipping point. Kathryn - who is also the sister of my late partner - sat down and with some effort put all the recipes together for easy reference.

This is an expanded version of that first Sten cookbook, which proved to be one of the more popular sites on my homepage. (http://www.acole.com)

I've pawed through my desk, come up with old Scotch-spattered Sten notes, and found more than a few recipes that were cut for space during the writing of the series.

And so, here it is: The Sten Cookbook.

Read, cook, eat and enjoy.

Stregg Forever, Allan Cole (Boca Raton, Fl. 2011)

Allan Cole

Recipes

Sten #1

The Book:

Vulcan is a factory planet, centuries old, Company run, ugly as sin, and unfeeling as death. Vulcan breeds just two types of native — complacent or tough. Sten is tough. When his family is killed in a mysterious accident, Sten rebels, harassing the Company from the metal world's endless maze-like warrens. He could end up just another burnt–out Delinq. But people like Sten never give up.

*****

The Eternal Emperor's Chili

(The following is the first cooking scene in the Sten series. The Emperor and his right hand Being, Col. Ian Mahoney, have some dire suspicions about what the CEO of Vulcan - one Baron Thoresen - is up to. Everything up to and including sending in the Imperial Guard is considered. As the Emperor considers his options, he puts together a very complicated recipe for killer chili. In the

end, a more subtle approach to the Thoresen problem is decided upon. It seems that the heat of the chili has helped put things in a cooler perspective.)

The Emperor, Mahoney decided, had finally gone mad. He was hovering over a huge bubbling pot half filled with an evil-looking mixture, muttering to himself.

"A little of this. A little of that. A little garlic and a little fat. Now, the cumin. Just a touch. Maybe a bit more. No, lots more." The Emperor finally noticed Mahoney and smiled. "You're just in time," he said. "Gimme that box."

Mahoney handed him an elaborately carved wooden box. The Emperor opened it and poured out a handful of long reddish objects. They looked like desiccated alien excrement to Mahoney.

"Look at these," he boasted to Mahoney, "Ten years in the biolabs to produce."

"What are they?"

"Peppers, you clot. Peppers."

"Oh, uh, great. Great."

"Don't you know what that means?"

Mahoney had to admit he didn't.

10

"Chili, man. Chili. You ain't got peppers, you got no chili."

"That's important, huh?"

The emperor didn't say another word. Just dumped in the peppers, punched a few buttons on his cooking console, then dipped up a huge spoonful of the mess and offered it to Mahoney.

He watched intently as Mahoney tasted. Not ba - then it hit him. His face went on fire, his ears steamed and he choked for breath.

The Emperor pounded him on the back, big grin on his face, and then offered him a glass of beer.

Mahoney slugged it down. Wheezed.

"Guess I got it just right," the Emperor said.

"You mean you did that on purpose?"

"Sure. It's supposed to scorch the hair off your butt. Otherwise it wouldn't be chili."

****

Now, if that isn't detailed enough for you, here's how you'd cook the Emperor's Chili in an early Twenty First Century Kitchen.

Allan Cole

The Ingredients

3 - 24 oz. cans kidney beans (drained)

16 oz. tomato sauce

12 oz. tomato paste

Too Much Garlic - 16 to 18 large cloves (diced)

2 large onions (chopped)

1 large green bell pepper (chopped)

1 large red bell pepper (chopped)

2 tablespoons fresh parsley (diced)

2 tablespoons ground cumin

2 tablespoons oregano

4 habaneros (deseeded, deveined and diced)

6 jalapenos (deveined, deseeded and diced)

1 pound steak (buffalo if you can get it) sliced

1 pound ground beef (buffalo if you can get it)

1 pound ground pork

4-6 bottles Guinness (more if you have invited witnesses)

One fifth Jose Cuervo Gold tequila.

Salt and pepper to taste (maybe 1/2 teaspoon each)

Allan Cole

Extra virgin olive oil - enough to sauté the ingredients - a couple of splashes.

****

The Directions

Sauté onions, garlic, peppers.

Put aside.

In same pan: lightly brown ground buffalo and ground pork.

Put aside.

In same pan, lightly brown steak slices.

In a large pot, bring to a simmer the tomato paste, tomato sauce, kidney beans, cumin, parsley, oregano, salt and pepper, habaneros and jalapenos.

Dump the whole mess in a crock pot.

Add half a bottle of Guinness.

Drink the other half.

Add one cup Jose Cuervo Gold tequila

(Go ahead, do a shot yourself.)

Slow cook for about 6 hours, adding more Guinness and Tequila to self as needed.

Serve with grated cheddar cheese and chopped onions.

Allan Cole

**Caution: Use quality spoons. Cheaper ones will dissolve.

****

Imperial Green Chili Cornbread

Chris and I got this recipe from Kathryn - his sister and my wife. It was cut for space, which was a pity since it goes so well with the chili.

The Ingredients

3/4 cup cornmeal

1 cup flour

3 teaspoons baking powder

1 cup milk

1 egg (well beaten)

1 tablespoon shortening (melted)

1 cup green chilies (chopped)

1 cup jack cheese (grated)

****

The Directions

Preheat oven to 425 degrees. Grease 8-inch square cake pan (or muffin pan). Mix cornmeal, flour and baking soda. Add milk, egg and shortening and blend well.

Stir in chilies and cheese.

Spoon into pan and bake for 25 to 30 minutes.

****

Prime World Margarita Recipe

This is another dish we intended to put in the chili scene. Margaritas are perfect to cool things down. But it didn't fit into the context of the scene with the Emperor and Mahoney. Then it got stuck aside and forgotten, until I pulled it out of the back of my desk, along with other ancient Sten notes.

It originally hailed from the bar/kitchen of our dear friend, Linda Beaty - a News Hen from way back (New York Times, LA Times, Wall Street Journal, etc.)who knows her spirits almost as well as she does the language.

Years ago we worked together on the copydesk of a Santa Monica newspaper and I remember mornings when she'd come in and announce to a room of shuddering reporters: "Death To All Modifiers," then sharpen a bank of pencils and go to work.

The Ingredients

1 part freshly squeezed lemon juice.

Allan Cole

2 parts Triple Sec

3 parts tequila

Add all ingredients. Chill. Salt the rim of the glasses and then serve with LOTS of ice.

Allan Cole

Sten #2
The Wolf Worlds

The Book:

Raised on the factory planet of Vulcan, Sten soon learns about the survival of the toughest. Now he wants more than survival. The Eternal Emperor rules countless worlds across the galaxy. Vast armies and huge fleets await his command. But when the Emperor needs to pacify the Wolf Worlds, the planets of the insignificant Lupus Cluster that have raised space piracy to a low art, he turns to his Mantis Team and its small band of militant problem–solvers. Sten's destiny is in his own hands.

A Bit More Backstory, Otherwise, Why Stregg?

Sten and his Mantis Team are dispatched by the Eternal Emperor to settle a religious dispute that is likely to end in all out warfare. Normally, the Emperor wouldn't have given a clot. The Lupus Cluster (known as The Wolf

Worlds) were on the edges of his empire. But, a mother lode of Iridium X - the stuff used to contain and control the super volatile AM2 - has been discovered and The Wolf Worlds are right in the path of all the greedy prospectors and mining companies sure to swarm there when word gets out.

But stopping the war will be no easy task. The trouble is there are three Pope-like beings who are at each other's throats. The Emp doesn't much care who comes out on top, as long as the conflict doesn't interrupt the mining companies who will hold his charter.

It is in the Wolf Worlds that we also introduce the Bhor - an incredibly violent breed of warriors whose favorite drink is Stregg - a booze so strong that the drinker's breath would stop a charging Banth in its tracks.

We didn't include a recipe for homemade Stregg in this novel, or any of the others, so by popular (really!) demand it is included here. As a special this week, we're also throwing in the recipe for The Emp's Old Time Corn Liquor.

But first:

18

Allan Cole

The Emperor's Salmon

Smiling to himself, Mahoney followed the Emperor. It was obvious his boss was having an excellent vacation. Mahoney hoped he'd be as happy once he finished Sten's report.

It was quite a campsite. A low, staked-down vee-tent almost into the bushes. A half-decayed log had been muscled up to a flat boulder. Stones had been piled nearby to form a three-sided fireplace.

Other than that, there were no signs that the Emperor had been camping in this spot for more than fifty years.

In the fireplace was tinder under a teepee-shaped collection of wood that went from twigs to some fairly sizable logs. The Eternal Emperor walked out of the brush, whistling softly. He was deftly bending a green sapling into a snowshoe-shaped grill. As he passed the fireplace he took out a disposable fire-stick, fired it, and pitched it at the wood. It roared into a four-foot pillar of flame.

"See that. Colonel? Good firebuilding. Woodsy lore and about half a gallon of petroleum. Now we wait for the fire to burn down, and I clean this here monster."

Allan Cole

Mahoney watched curiously as the Emperor took out a small knife and deftly cut the fish from below its gills to venthole. He carried the fish guts into the brush, then walked over to the riverbank to wash the now degutted salmon.

"Why don't you have one of the Gurkhas do that, sir?" Mahoney wondered.

"You'll never make a fisherman, Colonel, if you ask that question."

(The main scene continues, with Mahoney reporting the difficulties faced by Sten and his Mantis Team. Then:)

He walked to his tent and came back with a glassine jar full of a mildly brownish liquid. Mahoney looked at it suspiciously. One of the problems of being the Emperor's head of Secret Intelligence—Mercury Corps—and his confidant/aide/assassin was being subjected to the Imperial tastes for the primitive. Remembering a concoction called "chili," he shuddered.

"They called this 'shine,'" the Emperor explained. "Triple-distilled, which was easy. Run through the radiator

Allan Cole

of something those hillpeople called a fifty-three Chevy, which I never bothered finding out about. Then aged in a carbonized barrel for at least a day or so. Try it. It's an experience."

Mahoney lifted the jar. He figured the less the taste, the better off he'd be, and poured a straight gurgle down his throat.

He realized he'd never noticed that the river was a nova and that he seemed to be standing in the middle of the fireplace. But somehow he didn't drop the jar. Eyes watering, seeing double, he still managed to pass it to the Emperor.

"I see you're wearing a gun," the Emperor said sympathetically "Would you mind holding it on me while I have a drink?" Mahoney was still gasping as the Emperor chugged a moderate portion.

"Continue, Colonel, with your report. You are planning to stay for dinner, aren't you?"

Mahoney nodded. The Emperor smiled—he did hate to eat alone, and his Gurkkha bodyguards preferred their far simpler diet of rice, dhal, and soyasteak...

Allan Cole

(The Emperor reflects on the history of the Lupus Cluster, while Mahoney continues to fill him in. Then:)

The Emperor was busy dressing the fish. He'd picked a handful of berries from a bush on the outskirts of the clearing and a small clump of leaves from each of two bushes nearby.

"Juniper berries - they grow wild here; two local spices, basil and thyme, that I planted twenty years ago," he explained. He rubbed berry juices on both sides of the split salmon, then crushed the leaves and did the same…

(More reporting from Mahoney, who is getting hungrier by the minute. Finally:)

After the birchwood fire had burned down to coals, the Emperor put the salmon on the sapling grill. He'd left it for a few minutes, then quickly splashed corn liquor on the skin-side and skillfully flipped the slabs of fish over.

The fire flared and charred the skin, and then the Emperor extracted the fish.

Mahoney couldn't remember when he'd eaten anything better.

****

Allan Cole

If, unlike the Eternal Emperor, you don't own the Province Of Oregon, much less have your own fishing camp, here's a way you can prepare The Emperor's Salmon in a little getaway cabin, or in your own backyard.

The Ingredients

*1 bottle corn liquor (See Corn Liquor Recipe below or use Jim Beam)

1/2 cup honey

3 fresh bay leaves, diced

2 tablespoons peppercorns, crushed.

1 tablespoon sea salt

1 1/2 tablespoons juniper berries, crushed

* BBQ sauce (See The Emperor's BBQ Sauce)

2 pounds salmon filet, one side with skin on.

1 cedar plank, 16-by-8 inches

****

The Directions

Soak the cedar plank in water for about an hour.

Put one ounce of Corn Liquor into a shot glass and drink. Pass the bottle to companions, if any.

Allan Cole

Stir honey into one cup of corn liquor. In a large, shallow baking dish, combine the wine, the corn liquor and honey mixture with salt, bay leaves, peppercorns and juniper berries. Add the salmon, turn to coat and refrigerate for one hour.

Meanwhile, get your grill ready. Hickory Charcoal Briquettes are best. Mesquite, or pecan will do. Let the briquettes burn until they are covered with a nice, light gray ash. Put a throw away drip pan in the center and arrange the briquettes around the pan.

If you can do this without burning yourself, have another shot of corn liquor. If you can't, treat wound with a splash of corn liquor, then carefully measure out one ounce in a shot glass. Drink. It will ease the pain and steady the nerves for you to continue.

If you are using a gas grill - you lazy dog - turn off the center burner and no corn liquor for you! Okay, maybe a wee one.

Remove the salmon from the marinade, brush off the seasonings and lay the fish skin side down on the soaked cedar plank. Brush the salmon with olive oil and set the

Allan Cole

plank in the center of the cooking grate for indirect grilling. Cover and grill the salmon until just cooked, about 30 minutes; brush the salmon with the sauce during the last ten minutes of grilling.

Have another shot of corn liquor to steady your hands.

Then serve the salmon directly from the plank, heaping mounds of wild rice around it. Oh, you'll need the recipe for that, won't you?

****

The Emperor's Wild Rice

The Ingredients

Olive oil - Enough to sauté the vegetables and rice. Couple of tablespoons should do.

1 cup wild rice

3/4 cup celery - diced

1/4 cup carrots - diced

1 cup mushrooms - chopped

3 cups chicken broth (or vegetable broth)

1/4 teaspoon poultry seasoning (recipe below)

salt and pepper to taste

1/4 cup toasted slivered almonds

****

The Directions

Splash olive oil in large skillet. Sauté wild rice, onion, celery, carrots, and mushrooms until vegetables are golden brown. Add chicken (or vegetable) broth and poultry seasoning. Cover and simmer for 30 to 40 minutes, until the liquid is gone. (Don't burn the bottom. Watch carefully, tilting pan now and then to check for liquid.) Taste, then add salt and pepper if necessary. Top with toasted slivered almonds just before serving.

To toast nuts, spread out in a single layer on a baking sheet. Toast in a 350-degree oven, stirring occasionally, for 10 to 15 minutes. Or, toast in an ungreased skillet over medium heat, stirring, until golden brown and aromatic.

****

Quick Poultry Seasoning Recipe

2 teaspoons ground sage

1 1/2 teaspoons ground thyme

1 teaspoon ground marjoram

3/4 teaspoon ground rosemary

1/2 teaspoon nutmeg

Allan Cole

1/2 teaspoon finely ground black pepper

Mix them together and store the seasoning in a tight spice jar.

****

The Emp's Corn Liquor Recipe

The Ingredients

10 pounds whole kernel corn

5 gallons of warm water

1 cup yeast

The Directions

Put corn in a burlap bag. Wet with warmish water. Place bag in a warm dark place and keep moist for about ten days. When the sprouts are about a quarter-inch long the corn is ready.

Wash the corn, rubbing off the roots and sprouts.

Put the corn into your fermenter. (Yes, they have 'em at Amazon.com - http://tinyurl.com/3nnlph6)

Smash the corn, being damned sure all the kernels are cracked. (The "Jimmy Cracked Corn, And I Don't Care" song is a lot of drakh. We do care!)

Allan Cole

Boil 5 gallons of water and pour into fermenter with the smashed corn.

After the water cools add the yeast.

Seal and let age well for up to seven days.

After mash is fermented, use a wine filtering bag to remove the mash. Mahoney's great granddad used an old pillow case. His great granddad's great granddad used his old, worn out Long Johns. (Flap closed)

Pour into jug.

Drink. (Carefully and wisely and get yourself a designated driver, pal, this stuff is clotting lethal.)

Allan Cole

Sten #3
The Court Of A Thousand Suns

The Book:

Sten had fought his way up from slave labor on a factory world to commander of the Eternal Emperor's bodyguard, the Imperial Gurkhas. But during his first three months on Prime World, the most dangerous weapons Sten had encountered were the well–phrased lies of Court politicians.

It seemed no place for an honest fighting man. But when a bomb destroys a local bar, Sten discovers the danger and corruption behind Court intrigue.

Only quick work by Sten, Alex Kilgour, and a tough female detective can keep the Empire together and the Emperor alive.

A situation guaranteed to create many, many hangovers. And so we start with:

The Emperor's Angelo Stew

This is the first time we see Sten and The Eternal Emperor together. Our hero is new to the royal court and the Emperor has taken a rather fatherly interest in him. He's also testing him in many ways - some subtle, some not. One of the tests involves getting drunk together. But, Sten has to return to duty soon and to save him from the awful hangover sure to come - and also to sober him up - the Emperor introduces him to his favorite Sobriety Dish - Angelo Stew.

The Stew is named for the first chef who trained me. The real Angelo was one helluva chef - a few years and many pounds past retirement. The restaurateur who employed me was very kindly putting me through chef's school, but meanwhile I worked in his kitchen full time at night. Angelo was supposed to teach me some of his best dishes. Soon, I noticed that on certain sauces I could never match the taste of Angelo's wonderful concoctions. Puzzled, I watched even more closely. Then I realized that at crucial moments he was always sending me to fetch

30

things - like a Number 10 Can Of Tomatoes, or whatever.

Obviously he was adding certain spices while I was gone.

It took some nerve on my part to confront the wonderful -

but fierce - old Spanish gentleman, but when I did, he

sighed and confessed that he'd been unable to reveal

secrets he'd spent a lifetime learning. We got drunk

together that night, and he fixed me the stew to sober me

up before I left. After that, he treated me like a father

proudly imparting wisdom to a favored son.

****

"What the clot is Angelo stew?" Sten just had to ask.

"You don't need to know," the Emperor said.
"Wouldn't eat it if you did. Cures cancer...oh, we cured
that before, didn't we...Anyway...Angelo stew's the ticket.
Only thing I know will unfreeze our buttocks."

Sten watched as the Emperor worked. From what Sten
could gather, the first act of what was to be Angelo stew
consisted of thinly sliced chorizo - Mexican hard sausage,
the Emperor explained. The sausage and a heaping handful
of garlic were sautéed in Thai-pepper-marinated olive oil.

Allan Cole

Deliciously hot-spiced smells from the pan cut right through the Stregg fumes in Sten's nostrils.

The Emperor stopped his work and took a sip of Stregg. Smiled to himself, and tipped a small splash in with the chorizo. Then he went back to the task at hand, quartering four or five onions and seeding quarter slices of tomatoes.

He turned and pulled a half-kilo slab of bleeding red beef from a storage cooler and began chunking it up.

The Emperor shut off the flame under the sausage and garlic, started another pan going with more spiced oil, and tossed in a little sage, a little savory and thyme, and then palm-rolled some rosemary twigs and dropped those in on top. He stirred the mixture, considered a moment, then heaped in the tomato quarters and glazed them. He shut off the fire and turned back to Sten. He gave the young captain a long, thoughtful look and then began rolling the small chunks of beef into flour first, and then into a bowl of hot-pepper seeds.

He paused to turn the flame up under the sausage and garlic, then added the pepper-rolled beef as soon as the pan

Allan Cole

was hot enough. He stirred the beef around, waiting until it got a nice brown crust.

The Emperor finished the beef. He pulled out a large iron pan and dumped the whole mess into it. He also added the onions and tomatoes. Then he threw in a palmful of superhot red peppers, a glug or three of rough red wine, many glugs of beef stock, a big clump of cilantro, clanked down the lid, and set the flame to high. As soon as it came to a boil, he would turn it down to simmer for a while.

The stew was done now. The Emperor rose and ladled out two brimming bowlsful. Sten's mouth burst with saliva. He could smell a whole forest of cilantro. His eyes watered as the Emperor set the bowl in front of him. He waited as the man cut two enormous slices of fresh-baked sourdough bread and plunked them down along with a tub of newly churned white butter.

The Emperor spooned up a large portion of stew.

"Eat up, son. This stuff is great brain food. First your ears go on fire, then the gray stuff. Last one done's a grand admiral."

Allan Cole

Sten swallowed. The Angelo stew savored his tongue, and gobbled down his throat to his stomach. A small nuclear flame bloomed, and his eyes teared and his nose wept and his ears turned bright red. The Stregg in his bloodstream fled before a horde of red-pepper molecules.

"Whaddya think?" the Eternal Emperor said.

"What if you don't have cancer?" Sten gasped.

"Keep eating, boy. If you don't have it now, you will soon."

****

Stregg: How To Make Your Own

As mentioned previously, this heart-stopping booze appears first in Book Two: The Wolf Worlds, where a race of Viking-like beings is introduced. Hailing from an ice-planet, the ancestral enemy of the Bhor was the Streggan, a fierce beast that hunted them almost into annihilation. Finally, they turned the tide and wiped out the beast entirely. They named their favorite drink **Stregg**, in honor of their ancient enemy.

The name was inspired by a boozy session that Chris and I had at Harry's Bar in Century City, California. (We'd

34

Allan Cole

just made a big fat sale to ABC television.) There we discovered the wonders of Strega, the Italian liqueur. It means witch. If you drink it, you won't have to ask why.

To make Stregg for yourself, mix one part Strega and one part white tequila. Some prefer a little simple syrup. We did not.

****

Marr And Senn's Breakfast Party

Marr and Senn were among our favorite creations. They were Imperial Caterers who were at the center of every important social event on Prime World. They meet Sten for the first time in Court Of A Thousand Sun. They become fast friends -a friendship that will pay off in amazing ways as the series continues. Trivia: They are named for my sister-in-law, Vicky, a former prima ballerina. Her maiden name is Marsen.

Here's how we first described them in Court:

... In an age not generally known for permanent bondings, the two Milchen stood out. They had been sexually paired for more than a century and were passionately determined that the relationship should go on

Allan Cole

for a century more. However, such stability was not unusual in their species; for the Milchen of Frederick Two, pairing was literally for life — when one member of a Milchen pair died, the other would always follow within a few days. Long-term pairings among the Milchen were always of the same sex.

For want of a better description, call it male. The other gender — put the "female" label on it, it's easier — was called Ursoolas. Of all things in the many universes, the Ursoolas were among the most beautiful and delicate, beings of gossamer and many-changing perfumed colors. They lived only a few short months, and during that time it was all loving and sexual intensity. If a Milchen male pair was fortunate, it might enjoy two or three such relationships in its lifetime. Out of each bonding came a "male" pair and half-a-dozen dormant Ursoolas. The mother would whisper a few last loving words to her broodsac and then die, leaving the care of the young to the father pair.

For the Milchen, life was a never-ending breeding-cycle tragedy, that bred the kind of loneliness that can kill

36

a loving race. And so they evolved the only system open to them — same-sex bonding. Like most of their people, Marr and Senn were passionately devoted to each other, and to all other things of beauty.

They were slender creatures, a meter or so high, and covered with a downy, golden fur. They had enormous liquid-black eyes that enjoyed twice the spectrum of a human's. Their heads were graced with sensitive smelling antennae that could also caress like a feather. Their small monkeylike hands contained the Empire's most sensitive taste buds, and were largely the reason for Milchen's being among the Empire's greatest chefs. The Eternal Emperor himself grudgingly admitted they surpassed all other races in the preparation of fine meals. Except, of course, for chili.

****

The Breakfast Party

This is aimed at couples invited to stay over at Marr and Senn's palace. It's not Brunch - and is meant to be served around 10 a.m. (Prime World Time) The Milchens try to keep the guest list to just three or four couples. Naps

Allan Cole

after breakfast are encouraged. If Sten and the beauteous Detective Haines had tarried at Marr and Senn's palace, instead of spending the night at Haines' houseboat in the sky, this is the breakfast they would have enjoyed.

The Salad And Centerpiece:

Finely chop tomatoes, cucumbers, parsley, coriander, bell peppers, arugula and mint. Get the best olive oil you can find and mix with lemon juice and salt and pepper. Toss the salad with the dressing.

Dips - To Be Arrayed Around The Table:

These are available at most nicer markets, so don't kill yourself trying to make them from scratch. Remember, Marr and Senn have a big staff.

Tabouleh (Fresh veggies, oil and spices)

Creamy labaneh (sort of like cream cheese and yogurt)

Tahini (Sesame seeds and olive oil)

Hummus (Made from chick peas. Several varieties available. I like the garlic.)

Side Dishes:

Greek olives

Plenty of pita bread for scooping purposes

Allan Cole

Fresh pastries

Eggs Mediterranean:

Get out your largest skillet.

Finely chop handful of tomatoes, green onions, peppers, and garlic.

Sauté in pan.

Crack eight or more eggs into pan and cook them sunny side up.

Crumble big chunks of feta cheese (goat cheese) on top.

Place the entire pan in the center of the table.

Then invite your guests to scoop up whatever appeals to them with hunks of pita bread.

Serve with your favorite really strong coffee, Earl Grey tea with mint, orange juice and lemonade.

To Polish It Off:

Melt chocolate in a fondue pan.

Surround with fresh fruit - strawberries, sliced bananas, sliced apples - whatever strikes your fancy.

Let them dip away and eat.

Allan Cole

If you have a palace like Marr and Senn, send them all off for naps. If not, yawn widely and say as nicely as you can: "Don't you have homes to go to?" They'll get the hint and leave.

****

Son Of A Scrote Soufflé

Cliff Tarpy, the incredibly skilled assassin the Court Of A Thousand Suns, was a man of refined tastes. But if he'd been up extra late the night before on a particular difficult Kill, he'd revert to type - his family hailed from a rough and ready frontier planet - and would wade into a cholesterol sea for his breakfast. The following is a particular favorite. His cats liked it too.

The Ingredients

1 pound bacon, ham or sausage if you've got some (Turkey-based if you prefer)

10 large eggs

2 cups milk

Salt and pepper to taste

2 cups grated cheese

4-5 slices bread

Allan Cole

The Directions

Butter 9 x 13 inch pan. Cube any kind of bread and spread across bottom of pan. Fry a pound of bacon, ham or sausage if you've got some. Scatter more bread cubes on top. Beat 10 large eggs and 2 cups milk, salt and pepper. Pour over bread. Top with grated cheese. Chill overnight. Bake 1 hour at 300 degrees in pan of water.

Allan Cole

Sten # 4
Fleet Of The Damned

The Book:

Sten's luck seems to have deserted him. Having been assigned a tacdivision in the Fringe Worlds, he soon discovers that the Imperial Officers are more interested in having fun than honing their fighting skills. The enemy Tahn couldn't have picked a better time or place to launch their long–planned attack against the Empire. Sten and his men are outgunned and outmanned... But Sten isn't going to give up without a fight.

The Eternal Emperor's Picnic

The Eternal Emperor had definite ideas about a picnic.

A soft rain of five or ten minutes that ended just before the guests arrived added a sweetness to the air.

Said rain had been ordered and delivered.

He thought that a breeze with just a bit of an invigorating chill in it whetted appetites. As the day progressed, the breeze should become balmy, so the picnickers could loll under the shade trees to escape the warming sun.

Said gentle, shifting winds had also been ordered.

Last of all, the Eternal Emperor thought a barbecue the best form of all picnics, with each dish personally prepared by the host.

The Eternal Emperor scanned the vast picnic grounds of Arundel with growing disappointment as he added a final dash of this and splurt of that to his famous barbecue sauce. Meanwhile, all over the picnic grounds, fifty waldo cooks manning as many outdoor kitchen fires exactly copied his every dash and splurt.

Hundreds of years before, the Emperor's semi-annual barbecue had begun as a nonofficial event. He started it because he loved to cook, and to love to cook is to watch others enjoy what you have lovingly prepared. At first, only close friends were invited: perhaps 200 or so—a number he could easily handle with a few helpers. In fact,

43

Allan Cole

the Emperor believed there were many dishes that reached near perfection when prepared in quantities of this size: his barbecue sauce, for instance.

It was a simple event he could comfortably fit on a small shaded area of the fifty-five-kilometer grounds of his palace.

Then he had become aware of growing jealousy among the members of his court. Beings were irked because they felt they were not part of a nonexistent inner circle. His solution was to add to the guest list—which created a spreading circle of jealousy as far out as the most distant systems of his empire. The list grew to vast proportions.

Now, a minimum of 8,000 could be expected. There was no way the Emperor could personally prepare food in those proportions. The clotting thing was getting out of hand. It was in danger of becoming an official event—the likes of an Empire Day.

He had been tempted to end the whole thing. But the barbecue was one of the few social occasions he really enjoyed. The Eternal Emperor did not consider himself a good mixer.

Allan Cole

The solution to the cooking was simple: He had a host of portable outdoor kitchens built and the waldo cooks to tend them. Every motion he made, they duplicated, down to the smallest molecule of spice dusted from his hands. The solution to the now-official social nature of the event, however, proved impossible. So the Eternal Emperor decided to take advantage of it.

He invited only the key people in his empire to Prime World, and he used any potential jealousy of the uninvited to his advantage. As he once told Mahoney, "It's a helluva way to flush 'em out of the bush."

****

The Emperor's Barbecue Sauce

The Emperor sniffed his simmering sauce: Mmmmm...Perfect. It was a concoction whose beginnings were so foul-looking and smelling that Marr and Senn, his Imperial caterers, refused to attend. They took a holiday in some distant place every time he threw a barbecue.

The original creation was born in a ten-gallon pot. He always made it many days in advance. He said it was to give it time to breathe. Marr and Senn substituted "breed,"

45

but the Emperor ignored that. The ten gallons of base sauce was used sort of like sourdough starter - All he had to do was to keep adding as many ingredients as there were beings to eat it.

He dipped a crust of hard bread into the sauce and nibbled. It was getting better.

The secret to the sauce was the scrap meat. It had taken the Emperor years to convince his butchers what he meant by scrap. He did not want slices off the finest fillet. He needed garbage beef, so close to spoiling that the fat was turning yellow and rancid. The fact that he rubbed it well with garlic, rosemary, and salt and pepper did not lessen the smell. "If you're feeling squeamish," he always told Mahoney, "sniff the garlic on your hands."

The sauce meat was placed in ugly piles on racks that had been stanchioned over smoky fires - at this stage the recipe wanted little heat, but a great deal of smoke from hardwood chips. The Emperor liked hickory when he could get it. He constantly flipped the piles of meat so that the smoke flavor would penetrate. In this case, the

Allan Cole

chemistry of the near-spoiled scraps aided him: They were drying and porous and sucking at the air.

Then he - and his echoing waldoes - dumped the meat into the pot, filled it with water, and set it simmering with cloves of garlic and the following spices: three or more bay leaves, a cupped palm and a half of oregano, and a cupped palm of savory to counteract the bitterness of the oregano.

Then the sauce had to simmer a minimum of two hours, sometimes three, depending upon the amount of fat in the meat - the more fat, the longer the simmer.

While he was waiting for the meat to simmer to completion, he could drink many shots of Stregg and prepare the next part of the sauce at his leisure. At one time he invited a few friends to keep him company during this process, but in the end this created so many squabbles for the favor of his company that he declared that this was a sauce he must cook alone.

The sauce presented many possibilities in the choice of ingredients, but the Emperor liked using ten or more large onions, garlic cloves - always use too much

Allan Cole

garlic - chili peppers, green peppers, more oregano and savory, and Worcestershire sauce.

He sautéed all that in clarified butter. Then he dumped the mixture into another pot and set it to bubbling with a dozen quartered tomatoes, a cup of tomato paste, four green peppers, and a two-fingered pinch of dry mustard.

A health glug or three of very dry red wine went into the pot. Then he added the finishing touch. He stirred in the smoky starter sauce that he had prepared in advance, raised the heat, and simmered ten minutes.

The sauce was done.

****

Pitchfork Fondue

The Emperor's picnic wouldn't be complete without his famous fondue for the masses. With so many thousands of guests to feed, he had to think big. Okay, so here's big. (This recipe courtesy of our friends, Jonathan and Linda Beaty at A-Spear Ranch in New Mexico. The nearest town: Truth Or Consequences. A fitting name for what follows.)

Allan Cole

The Implements

1 giant cast iron kettle on a tripod. (Spread out as many others as you might need around the castle grounds, with sufficient 'bot and waldoes to handle the job.)

1 sieve wired to a long stick or pole

3 - three-prong pitchforks

The Ingredients

60 pounds ground kidney suet

300 New York steaks - six to eight ounces. No thicker than 1/2 inch.

The Directions

Build a campfire and let burn down to hot coals.

Have your friendly town butcher grind the suet. You can substitute oil or Crisco if preferred.

Bring suet to a rolling boil. Boil to remove all moisture out of the suet, skimming particles from the surface of the fat with the sieve wired to the long stick. When all the moisture has boiled out, the fat will become smooth and no longer bubble.

Allan Cole

Spear three steaks at a time - one on each prong. Hold pitchfork in hot fat about one minute for rare, not more than one and a half minutes for medium.

Serves: 300

****

Garlic Roasted Potatoes

Perfect to accompany a BBQ, or just to nosh on while floating in your Prime World houseboat in the Sky. Sour cream's nice. So's butter.

The Ingredients

Potatoes - as many as there are people

Diced garlic - a palmful for each potato

Extra virgin olive oil - About a tablespoon for each potato

The Directions

Poke fork holes in the potatoes.

Drizzle olive oil over each baker.

Heap diced garlic on each one.

Bake at 355 degrees (F) until crusty on the outside and soft on the inside. About an hour.

****

Allan Cole

The Emperor's Bean There, Done That Salad

The Ingredients

1 15-oz. can black beans, rinsed and drained

1 15-oz. can kidney beans, drained

1 15-oz. can cannellini beans, drained and rinsed

1 green bell pepper, chopped

1 red bell pepper, chopped

10 oz. of corn kernels. Fresh from the cob or frozen.

1 red onion, chopped

1 habanero chili - Seeded, ribbed and diced

1/2 cup olive oil

1/2 cup red wine vinegar

2 tablespoons fresh lime juice

1 tablespoon lemon juice

2 tablespoons white sugar

1 tablespoon salt

1 clove crushed garlic

1/4 cup chopped fresh cilantro

1/2 tablespoon ground cumin

1/2 tablespoon ground black pepper

1 dash hot pepper sauce

Allan Cole

1/2 teaspoon chili powder

The Directions

In a large bowl, combine beans, bell peppers, corn, red onion and habanero chili.

In a small bowl, whisk together olive oil, red wine vinegar, lime juice, lemon juice, sugar, salt, garlic, cilantro, cumin, and black pepper. Season to taste with hot sauce and chili powder.

Pour olive oil dressing over vegetables; mix well. Chill thoroughly and serve cold.

Allan Cole

Sten #5
Revenge Of The Damned

The Book:

Sten had fully expected to die in a blaze of glory, taking the Emperor's greatest foe with him. Instead, he ended up a slave laborer in a POW camp deep in the heart of enemy territory. But sitting out the action had never been Sten's style. And now that the war was building to a climax, the Eternal Emperor needed him more than ever. Not even the toughest prison in the known universe can keep Sten from his mission…

****

The Emperor's Nuked Hen

The Emperor was preparing a dinner that he had promised Mahoney was perfectly suited to a war motif. He called it "nuked hen".

Using his fingers and the hollow of his palm as measuring spoons, he dumped the following ingredients into a bowl: a pinch of fresh cayenne, two fingers of ground salt, ground pepper, a palm of dried sage, and finely diced horseradish. He moved the bowl over to his big black range. Already sitting beside it was a bottle of vodka, fresh-squeezed lime juice, a half cup of capers and a tub of butter.

The Emperor took a fat Cornish game hen out of a cold box and placed it on the metal table. He found a slim-bladed boning knife, tested the edge, and then nodded in satisfaction. He turned the hen over, back side up, and started his first cut alongside the spine.

He picked up his knife. "You might want to watch this, Ian," he said. "Boning a hen is easy when you know how, but you can chop the clot out of it and yourself if you don't."

Very carefully, the Emperor cut on either side of the spine. He pushed a finger through the slit and pulled the bone up through the carcass. Next, he laid the hen flat,

Allan Cole

placed a hand on either side of the spine, and crunched down with his weight.

"See what I mean?" he said as he lifted the breastbone out.

The Emperor moved over to his range and fired up a burner.

"First, I'm going to burn the clot out of this hen," the Emperor said, turning to his range. "The whole trick is getting your pan hot enough."

The Emperor turned the flame up as high as it would go and then slammed on a heavy cast-iron pan. In a few moments, the pan began to smoke, and fans in the duct above the range whirred on. A few moments more, and the pan stopped smoking.

"Check the air just above the fan," the Emperor said. "It's getting wavery, right?"

"Right."

"As the pan gets hotter, the air will wave faster and faster until the whole interior is a steady haze."

The haze came right on schedule.

"So it's ready now?" Mahoney asked.

Allan Cole

"Almost, but not quite. This is the place most people foul up. In a minute or two the haze will clear and the bottom of the pan should look like white ash."

As soon as the ashen look appeared, the Emperor motioned for Mahoney to duck back. Then he dipped out a big chunk of butter, dumped it into the pan, and moved out of the way. Mahoney could see why as flames flashed above the pan. As soon as they died down, the Emperor moved swiftly forward and poured the spices out of the bowl and into the pan. He gave the mixture a few stirs in one direction, then the other. Next he tossed in the Cornish game hen. A column of smoke steamed upward in a roar.

"I give it about five minutes each side," the Emperor said. "Then I spread capers all over it and toss the hen into the oven for twenty minutes or so to finish it off."

The Emperor dumped the thoroughly blackened hen into a baking dish. On went the capers, and into the oven it went - at 350 degrees. He cranked the flames down on the range, shoved the pan of drippings back on the fire, and stirred in two Imperial glugs of vodka and a quarter glug of

Allan Cole

lime juice. He would use the mixture to glaze the hen when it came out of the oven.

"I sort of get the idea," Mahoney said, "that you're in the process of heating up a pan for the Tahn."

The Emperor's Asparagus-Normandy

He slid the nuked hens from the oven and slid them neatly onto a platter. He said, "The trouble is, that it's been so long since we've had a real war folks forget that war hurts."

"The Mueller Wars," Mahoney supposed. "I guess that was the last of any size."

The Emperor got a thick square package from the Fresh and dumped it onto the counter. He poked the wrapping with a finger, leaving an indentation.

"We're getting soft, that's out trouble," he said. "We've been letting things go on to long... giving the Tahn too much time for a buildup."

He unwrapped the packet, revealing a lump of white cheese. "It's Neufchatel cheese," he informed Mahoney, "from a place on Earth they used to call Normandy. Beautiful beaches, until they got polluted. But, before that, a whole lot of men learned just how much war can hurt on those beaches."

Mahoney grimaced, remembering their own bloodbath on the battleship Normandie... which is where all the trouble with the Tahn really got started. Never occurred to him that the ship had been named after some bloody incident only the Emperor knew about. Or that some cream cheese looking thingie came from there.

By now the Emperor was onto the next step. Green spears of asparagus came out. Twelve of them, Mahoney noted for future reference. Then he fetched out a flat container of something that was labeled "Prosciutto."

"I sliced it up real nice before," the Emperor said. He took a piece of some kind of pinkish meat so thinly cut that it was transparent. He offered it to Mahoney. "Go, ahead. Try it."

Mahoney did. He was not surprised to find that it was delicious. Very tender, with a delicate smoky flavor.

"You have no idea how many years it took me to duplicate that," the Emperor said. "It's just ham, Italian style. But, that's what makes the whole difference. In my

Allan Cole

book, the greatest thing the Italians ever created wasn't Rome but prosciutto."

****

Further Hen and Asparagus Details:

If you became too engrossed in the Emperor's problems with the Tahn to pay attention,, here's the quick and easy way to do both dishes.

The Ingredients - Nuked Hens

Figure half a Cornish game hen per person. A whole one if one of the person is extra hungry. If your butcher won't bone them for you, at least get him/her/it to cut them in half.

Cumin

Sage

Horse radish (fresh)

Capers

Salt

Pepper

Butter

Lime juice

Vodka

Allan Cole

The Directions

Start getting a cast iron pan nice and hot.

Meanwhile, pre-heat your oven to 350 degrees (F)

Grease a roasting pan - use olive oil if you like.

In a bowl, put a 1/4 teaspoon of Cumin. One tablespoon of sage. One tablespoon of finely diced horseradish. One quarter teaspoon of ground pepper. Salt to taste. I like adding diced garlic, some people don't.

Mix ingredients well.

Rub game hens with the above mixture.

Dump two tablespoons of butter into the hot pan. More if needed.

Slap in the game hens. About five minutes on each side. Poking around so they don't stick.

Put the game hens in the greased roasting pan. Cover with a foil tent.

Bake at 350 for about an hour. Uncover and finish off. Be patient - make sure there is no pink around the bones.

The Ingredients - Asparagus

1/2 pound prosciutto, sliced

8 oz. Neufchatel cheese, softened

Allan Cole

12 spears fresh asparagus, trimmed

The Directions

Preheat oven to 450 degrees F.

Spread prosciutto slices with Neufchatel cheese. Wrap slices around two or three asparagus spears. Arrange wrapped spears in a single layer on a medium baking sheet.

Bake 15 minutes in the preheated oven, until asparagus spears are tender.

****

Rykor's Seaside Antipasto

Rykor is everyone's favorite spook shrink. The walrus-like being serves as head of Mercy Corps psi-war department, and as such one of the Emperor's key consultants and all matters involving dirty tricks.

Here's how we first introduced her in Sten #1:

****

Rykor, too, was happy. Wild arctic seas boomed in her mind. Waves climbed toward the gray, overcast sky as glaciers calved huge bergs.

She rolled as she surfaced, exultantly spouting, then crashed her flukes against the water, and leapt free from wave to wave in powerful, graceful dives. There was a gentle tap on her shoulder.

Rykor rolled one eye open and sourly looked up at Frazer, one of her assistants. "You want?" she rumbled.

"There's a vid for you. From Prime World."

Rykor whuffled through her whiskers and braced both arms on the sides of the tank. She levered her enormous bulk up and over into the gravchair. Folds of blubber slopped over the sides until the frantic chair tucked them all safely in place. She tapped controls, and the chair slid her across the chamber to the main screen. Frazer fussed beside her.

"It's in reference to that new Guards recruit. The one you put the personal key on."

"Figures," Rykor muttered. "Now I'll get more walrus jokes. Whatever a walrus is."

The screen was blank, except for a single line of blinking letters. Rykor was mildly surprised, but touched

Allan Cole

the CIPHER button, and added the code line. She motioned Frazer away from the screen.

It cleared, and Mahoney beamed out at her.

"Thought I'd take a moment of your time, Rykor, and ask you to check on one of my lads."

Rykor touched a button, and a second screen lit. "Sten?"

"Now that'd be a good guess."

****

She has other attributes as well. Consider: You know how it is when you're just too clottin' tired to cook? Your feet are dragging and your brain is on empty? Well, during the Tahn Wars, things got pretty wearisome for the Eternal Emperor, too. His place of last refuge for good talk and a meal was Rykor. Rykor's specialty was a marvelous bivalve, shrimp and squid antipasto. Here's how she made it:

To Be Sautéed

5 pounds mussels in shells

5 pounds clams in shells

1 cup shallots - Sliced

Allan Cole

3 cloves garlic - Sliced

6 sprigs of fresh thyme

1/4 cup extra virgin olive oil

1 1/2 cups dry white wine

For The Marinade

1 cup diced red peppers

1 tablespoon chopped fresh thyme

2 tablespoons extra-virgin olive oil

Salt and pepper, to taste

****

To complete The Salad

4 tablespoons olive oil, divided

1 pound jumbo shrimp, peeled, tails on

1 pound frozen squid (tentacles and rings), thawed

1 large head romaine, washed and drained

1 cup diced, peeled cucumber (about 1 large cucumber)

****

For Garnish

A nice Italian bread, grilled with garlic and olive oil, then cubed

Allan Cole

Mozzarella cheese - cubed

Lemon wedges

****

The Directions

Sort clams and mussels. Toss any that are open. Scrub the rest.

Heat oil - medium flame - in a large pan. Add shallots, garlic and thyme. Sauté until shallots are translucent.

Add clams and wine. Cover and simmer until all clams are open - about six minutes.

Remove clams (turn off pan) and toss any that didn't open.

Keep 1 pound for garnish. Refrigerate. Shuck the meat from the rest.

Repeat with the mussels - tossing out those that don't open. Refrigerate one pound for garnish. Shuck the meat and add to the same bowl with clams.

Add red peppers, thyme and olive oil to the clams and mussels and toss.

Salt and pepper to taste, then cover and refrigerate.

Allan Cole

Get the skillet going again, heating one tablespoon of olive oil. Add the shrimp, grilling until opaque. Spoon them out on a plate.

Back to the skillet. Grill the squid in olive oil until done - about three or four minutes.

Spoon it onto the plate with the shrimp.

Chop romaine into bite-sized pieces and put into a large chilled bowl.

Add cucumbers, two tablespoons of olive oil, salt and pepper to taste. Toss.

Arrange shrimp, squid, clams and mussels artfully in and around the lettuce. Add some cherry tomatoes, black olives and lemon wedges for color.

But wait!

Don't forget the clams and mussels you put in the fridge. Stick them into the salad, here and there and anywhere.

Garnish with grilled Italian garlic bread and mozzarella cheese.

Dig in.

Allan Cole

Rykor's Green Tea-Lacquered Salmon

(With Sweet Potatoes and Spinach)

Here's another Rykor favorite. But you have to shoot her a fins-up via her comline a couple of E-days in advance.

The Ingredients

Make one cup of green tea. (fresh leaves only, please)

4 teaspoons honey

4 fillets salmon

4 tablespoons extra virgin olive oil

4 sweet potatoes, peeled and diced

8 cups baby spinach

2 tablespoons garlic, minced. Three if you really like garlic.

1 shallot, minced. Two is okay.

4 large shiitake mushrooms - Remove stems. Slice in half.

1/2 cup dry white wine

2 tablespoons lemon juice

1 cup chicken broth

2 teaspoons thyme leaves, chopped fine

Allan Cole

The Directions

Nestle salmon in a lightly oiled broiling pan. Brush with honey and tea. Pour any remaining tea around the fish. Marinate in the refrigerator, covered, 1 hour or up to 2 days.

Heat 3 tablespoons of the olive oil in a skillet over medium heat. Add the sweet potatoes; cook, stirring, until golden, 6-10 minutes. Transfer to a bowl. Cover.

Add the spinach and garlic to the skillet. Cook, stirring, until the spinach is just wilted, less than 1 minute. Transfer to a shallow serving bowl. Cover.

Heat broiler. Line a broiler pan with foil. Spritz with canola or olive oil cooking spray. Place the salmon in the pan skin side-down; season with 1/4 teaspoon of the salt. Broil until golden, about 2 minutes.

Lower the heat to 350 degrees. (F)

Bake salmon until just cooked through, 5-10 minutes.

Pour remaining tablespoon of the oil into the skillet. Heat over medium heat; add shallots and shiitakes. Cook, stirring, until the shallots are translucent and the

Allan Cole

mushrooms have begun to release some of their juices, 3-4 minutes.

Add wine and lemon juice, stirring to scrape up browned bits. Heat over medium-high heat until reduced by half, about 3 minutes; add the chicken stock. Reduce by half - about 3 minutes.

Add thyme, remaining 1/4 teaspoon of the salt and pepper to taste.

Pour mushroom and shallot mixture over spinach.

Top with salmon.

Serve with sweet potatoes.

Allan Cole

Sten #6
The Return Of The Emperor

The Book:

The Eternal Emperor was dead, and the five members of the Privy Council ruled in his place. But they quickly discovered that their power would collapse around them if they didn't locate the Emperor's secret source of Anti–Matter Two, the economic keystone of the Empire.

And so they sent a team of crack commandos to capture Sten, one of their late ruler's few surviving confidantes.

But Sten, as usual, had his own agenda. For he knew something about the Eternal Emperor that would shake the Empire to its foundations.

To play his part, all Sten had to do was kill the five most powerful beings in the universe...

Raschid's Eggs of Pattipong

Pattipong described them on the menu as Imperial Eggs Benedict. For some reason, the name bothered Raschid. He argued - mildly. Pattipong told him to get back to the kitchen. "Imperial good name. Thailand...best elephants. Royal Elephants. Or so I hear."

Raschid had made sourdough starter a week or so before - warm water, equal amount of flour, a bit of sugar, and yeast. Cover in a nonmetallic dish and leave until it stinks.

He used that as a base for what were still called English muffins. They were equally easy to make. For about eight muffins, he brought a cup of milk to a boil, then took it off the stove and dumped in a little salt, a teaspoon of sugar, and two cupfuls of premixed biscuit flour. After he beat it all up, he let it rise until double size; then he beat in another cup of flour and let the dough rise once more.

Then open-ended cylinders were half filled with the dough. Raschid did not mention that the short cylinders had been pet food containers with both ends cut off. Even in this district, somebody might get squeamish.

He brushed butter on his medium-hot grill and put the cylinders down. Once the open end had browned for a few seconds, he flipped the cylinder, browned the other side and lifted the cylinder away, burning fingers in the process.

He added more butter and let the muffins get nearly black before putting them on a rack to cool. For use - within no more than four hours - he would split them with a fork and toast them.

He next found the best smoked ham he - or rather Pattipong - could afford. It was thin-sliced and browned in a wine-butter-cumin mixture.

Raschid went back to his recipe. The browned ham was put in a warming oven. He had lemon juice, red pepper, a touch of salt, and three egg yolks waiting in a blender. He melted butter in a small pan.

Then his mental timer went on. Muffins toasted...eggs went into boiling water to poach...the muffins were ready...ham went on top of the muffins...two and a half

Allan Cole

minutes, exactly, and the eggs were plopped on top of the ham.

He flipped the blender on and poured molten butter into the mixture. After the count of twenty, he turned the blender off and poured the hollandaise sauce over the eggs.

"Voila, Sr. Pattipong."

****

Raschid's All Purpose Spice

When Raschid - The Emperor's Alter Ego - worked in Pattipong's spaceport diner, he would have needed a good all purpose spice to dash on just about everything while cooking.

This is a recipe taught to me by an old chef many, many years ago. I keep a shaker of it on hand in my own kitchen. Always meant to put it in one of the Stens, but never got around to it.

The Ingredients

1 1/2 tablespoons onion powder

3 tablespoons garlic powder

3 tablespoons (Hatch) chili powder

1 tablespoon dried oregano

1 tablespoon dried thyme

2 1/2 tablespoons paprika

Combine ingredients and put in a shaker.

Spaceport Meatloaf

This is a slow-cooker recipe for a stick-to-your-ribs dinner for hardworking crewmen. The original recipe was Pattipong's, but Raschid improved on it.

The Ingredients

1-1/2 pounds lean ground beef. (I also like turkey, and ground buffalo when I can get it.)

3 large spicy Italian sausages. (Turkey-based for the diet conscious.)

1/2 cup seasoned dry bread crumbs

1/2 cup cheddar cheese. (Reduced fat kind, if you like. Or even soy-based.)

2 eggs, lightly beaten (Or the Egg-Beater equivalent.)

1/2 cup onion - minced.

4 garlic cloves - minced

1/2 cup mushrooms - minced

Two tablespoons Raschid's All-Purpose Spice (See the recipe above.)

The Directions

Dump everything into a bowl and starting mushing the ingredients with your hands. Really get into it. This is great therapy.

Form into a loaf.

Place on foil, sprayed with Pam. (I like the olive oil kind)

Insert the whole loaf into the crockpot. Cover and cook on low for about six hours. Lift the whole thing out, using the handy-dandy foil ends.

Slice and serve with some big bottles of catsup and hot sauce.

****

Spaceport Mashed Taters

Naturally, you're going to want some mashed potatoes to go with the meat loaf.

The Ingredients

3 1/2 pounds russet potatoes

2 tablespoons sea salt

2 cups chicken broth. (I get the low sodium kind.)

6 cloves garlic, crushed

6 oz. grated Parmesan

The Directions

Peel and dice potatoes. Dump the whole mess into a large saucepan, add the salt, and cover with water. Bring to a boil, then reduce heat to maintain a rolling boil. Cook until potatoes fall apart when poked with a fork.

Heat the chicken broth and the garlic medium heat until simmering. Remove from heat and set aside.

Drain the potatoes. Mash and add the garlic-broth mixture and Parmesan; stir to combine.

****

Raschid's Roasted Corn

The Ingredients

As many ears of corn as you have hungry beings to serve. Leave the husk on.

Olive oil spray

Raschid's All-Purpose Spice

The Directions

Peel back the husks from the corn.

Allan Cole

Spritz with olive oil.

Dust with Raschid's All-Purpose Spice.

Enclose the ears of corn in their husks again.

Place on a sheet of foil in an oven heated to 350 degrees.

Roast 35 minutes.

Serve in the husks.

Dusable's Hot Dog Classic

The next stage of the Emperor's return journey - still in his Rashid guise - takes him to a planet called Dusable. A world where it is All Politics, All The Time. Obviously it is named after one of the suburbs of Chicago. The Emp's adventures there were inspired by crooked politicians and ward bosses everywhere - especially Old Chicago. Which, is pretty much like the New Chicago, but older.

We wrote a little scene in the Dusable section that featured Raschid re-creating the classic Chicago Hot Dog - arguably the best there is. Our editor at Del Rey was already on us for that section taking up to much space, so we grudgingly cut it.

Allan Cole

Here it is back again.

The Ingredients

1 all-beef hot dog (buy the best you can)

1 poppy seed hot dog bun (again, don't go cheap - get the best)

1 tablespoon yellow mustard (Dijon)

1 tablespoon sweet green pickle relish

1 tablespoon chopped onion

4 tomato wedges - get really ripe ones

1 dill pickle spear - from your deli, not the jar

2 hot peppers

1 dash celery salt

The Directions

Boil water. Reduce heat to low, place hot dog in water, and cook 5 minutes or until done. Remove hot dog and set aside.

Carefully place a steamer basket into the pot and steam the hot dog bun 2 minutes or until warm.

Place hot dog in the steamed bun. Pile on the toppings in this order: yellow mustard, sweet green pickle relish,

Allan Cole

onion, tomato wedges, pickle spear, sport peppers, and celery salt.

The tomatoes should be nestled between the hot dog and the top of the bun. Place the pickle between the hot dog and the bottom of the bun. I like them with catsup, but if I were in Chicago and did that, I'd be shot.

Allan Cole

Sten #7
Vortex

The Book:

The Empire is in chaos. The once–great Imperial Navy has been shattered in battle and lies burning in space, riven by a civil war that threatens to engulf humanity's future. For the revered Eternal Emperor is not the man his subjects thought him to be — and may not even be human at all. And it is Sten — Imperial bodyguard, spy, assassin, renegade — who now leads humanity's fight for survival. Taking command of the last rebel fleet, he sets out on a desperate quest to seek and destroy the dark source of his former master's power.

Denounced as a traitor, hunted by forces loyal to the Emperor, Sten must risk everything to annihilate the Empire he vowed to protect.

The Emperor's Bombay Birani

"The theme tonight is India," the Eternal Emperor said.

The Emperor held up a mound of cubed meat. About two pounds worth, Sten noted.

"This is goat," the Emperor said. "I had a field constructed for him and his brothers and sisters. Had the field planted with the same stuff his ancestors ate in India - mint, wild onion, you name it." He plunked the mass into an ovenproof casserole.

He started shaking out spices over the goat. "A little ginger," he said, shifting to the recipe again. "Ground cloves, cardamom, chili, cumin...heavier than the others...couple of squeezes of garlic, and ye olde salt and pepper."

He dumped in some yogurt and lemon juice, and stirred up the whole mess, then set it to the side. He started frying onions in peanut oil.

He dumped half the fried onions on the lamb and mixed it up. He pulled the rice off the range. The water had been boiling for about five minutes. He drained the rice, stirred it up with the onions, and spread it out over the lamb.

"A little butter drizzled on the top," the Emperor said, "and...voila! I call this Bombay Birani, but basically it's an old goat stew." He slammed on a tight-fitting lid, popped the casserole into the oven, and set it for bake.

"Now, I'm going to cheat," the Emperor said. "The way this is supposed to go is, you set it at 380 degrees. Bake one hour. Then cut it to 325 and go for an hour more."

"But Marr and Senn, bless their souls, have come up with a new oven. Cuts real time half or more. And I can't tell the difference."

(A few story points are made and then...)

It was an incredible dinner. Unforgettable. As usual.

There were mounds of food all over the table. Dhal and cucumber cooler. Three kinds of chutney: green mango, Bengal, and hot lime. Real hot lime.

Little dishes of extra hot sauces and tiny red peppers. And fresh griddled flat bread - chapatties, the Emperor called them. Plus the Bombay Birani.

Fragrant steam rose from the casserole.

Allan Cole

"Dig in," the Emperor said.

Sten dug.

****

Goat Curry, Mon

(Here's a Jamaican Slow-Cooker Twist on what is essentially the same dish.)

The Ingredients

4 pounds goat meat, cut into bite sized pieces or chunks

3 large carrots, chopped

3 large onions, chopped

3 scotch bonnet peppers, minced

(If you want less heat remove the membrane from the peppers.)

3 1/2 cups chicken stock or beef stock

1 cup coconut milk

1 teaspoon allspice

1 teaspoon salt to taste

1 black pepper to taste

1 teaspoon red pepper flakes

About 5 tablespoons curry powder (add more or less to taste)

Allan Cole

2 large garlic cloves, minced

1/4 cup lemon juice

2 tablespoons olive oil

The Directions

This calls for a large bowl to start with. In it, combine the goat, two onions, scotch bonnet peppers, red pepper flakes, allspice, salt and pepper, and three tablespoons of (Jamaican) curry powder. Dig in with both hands, my friends, working the mixture well. Some call this "marrying" the ingredients. Maybe - but you should at least get very clotting friendly. Cover the bowl with saran wrap and place it in the refrigerator to marinate overnight.

The next day, remove the blissfully marinated goat and spices from the refrigerator and set aside.

In a heated skillet, add two tablespoons of extra virgin olive oil. Lightly cook the remaining two tablespoons of curry. Just a few minutes. Stirring, and being careful not to burn it. Then, using tongs, fish out the goat meat and brown it on all sides.

Put the browned meat in a crock pot.

Allan Cole

Add the marinated spices and vegetables to the skillet, stirring so they don't stick. Then add the rest. Cook until the onions are caramelized.

Put it all in the crock pot and mix well.

Finally, bring the stock, the stock, the coconut milk and the lemon juice to a boil.

Pour the mixture over the goat meat.

Cover and cook on "low" for six to eight hours.

****

The Emperor's Jerk Chicken

From the following, you can tell that Chris and I were really trying to work a Reggae-world sort of theme into Vortex. We wrote most of a whole section, then decided it took us nowhere.

But, here's a recipe we collected for the abandoned section. (Hmm. Maybe that's where some of Kilgour's missing jokes went. Gotta dig through my desk a little more.)

Anyway, try the following. I know you'll enjoy it.

The Ingredients

1 large onion, cut into chunks

Allan Cole

3 teaspoons chopped ginger

1 habanero pepper. Seed it. Cut away the ribs. Mince.

2 teaspoons ground allspice

2 tablespoons dry mustard

2 tablespoons honey

1 teaspoon freshly ground black pepper

2 tablespoons red wine

2 tablespoons soy sauce - I use the reduced sodium version.

5 cloves garlic. Minced.

3 pounds chicken breast or thigh. (Or, combine both cuts. The thigh meat keeps the breast from getting too dry.)

The Directions

Combine onion and ginger in a blender. Zap it until finely chopped.

Add remaining ingredients, except chicken, and pulse until well blended.

Place chicken in a crock pot and douse with the sauce. Cover, set on low, and cook for 6 to 8 hours. or until chicken is tender.

****

Allan Cole

Rykor's Saucy Scallops

Things get really bad in Vortex. So much so that Rykor dreams of the good old days on her home world where the scallops were fat and plentiful. Here's her favorite recipe:

The Ingredients - For The Scallops

1 pound sea scallops

1 tablespoon extra virgin olive oil

1 tablespoon butter. (I use one of the faux butters. The old ticker, you know.)

The Ingredients - For The Sauce

3 tablespoons butter

2 tablespoons minced shallots

2 tablespoons minced parsley (Flat leaf variety if you can get it.)

2 tablespoons minced chives

1/4 tablespoon lemon zest

1/2 cup dry white wine

The Directions - Scallops First

Wash and pat the scallops dry. (And I mean dry)

Season them with salt and pepper. (I skip the salt)

Allan Cole

Heat a 12-inch medium skillet until it's a medium temperature.

Melt the butter.

Add the olive oil.

When they are both warmed through add the scallops.

Brown the scallops on both sides - about two to four minutes per side.

Put aside in a warm dish.

The Directions - The Sauce

Using the same skillet, melt half the remaining butter.

Sauté the shallots about one minute.

Add the wine and simmer for about four minutes - until it is reduced by half.

Add the chives, parsley and lemon zest.

Reduce heat to low and whisk in the remaining butter until the sauce thickens.

Finishing It Off

Return the scallops to the pan and stir about until all the pieces are nicely coated and warmed through.

Serve with steamed rice and The Emperor's Asparagus Normandy.

Allan Cole

Sten #8
Empire's End

The Book:

At last! The explosive finale of Sten's adventures as the Eternal Emperor's most trusted friend, bodyguard, troubleshooter...and assassin!

See Sten undertake the ultimate treasure hunt, as he and his comrades seek out the source of the Eternal Emperor's power: Anti-Matter Two. Learn the secret of the Eternal Emperor's past: Who is he? Where did he come from? And how did he become immortal?

Watch as the loyal Sten turns traitor at last, turning on the Eternal Emperor to save his own skin...and the Empire itself! Eternity is doomed to end.

And if Sten has his way, it will end sooner rather than later!

Sten's Ultimate Steak Sandwich

Sten was rather morosely preparing himself a solitary meal, trying to remind himself that the best revenge is living well. Yet another pastime he had sort of picked up from the Eternal Emperor.

His meal was, by description, a simple Earth sandwich. Its filling would be a rib-eye steak from a steer.

But it may have been the Ultimate Steak Sandwich.

Earlier that day, before the paperwork and Go Higher And Hither orders had a chance to consume him as usual, he'd cut diagonal slices in the three-centimeter piece of meat. The steak went into a marinade - one-third extra-virgin olive oil, two-thirds Guinness - the remarkable dark beer he had been introduced to just before his last face-to-face meeting with the Eternal Emperor - salt, pepper, and a bit of garlic.

Now it was ready for the charbroiler.

He took softened butter, and beat a teaspoon of dried parsley, a teaspoon of tarragon, a teaspoon of thyme, and a teaspoon of oregano into it. He spread the butter on a

Allan Cole

freshly baked soft roll, foil-wrapped the roll, and put the roll in to warm.

Next he sliced onions. A lot of onions. He sautéed them in butter and paprika. As they started to sizzle, he warmed, in a double broiler, a half liter of sour cream mixed with three tablespoons of horseradish.

Next he'd charbroil the steak just until it stopped moving, slice it on the diagonal, put the meat on the roll, onions on the meat, sour cream on the onions, and commit cholesterolicide.

For a side dish he had thin-sliced garden tomatoes with a vinegar/olive oil/basil/thin-chopped chive dressing and beer.

****

Marr and Senn's Dinner Party

Sten wiped chicken gore on his apron and took the message from the runner. He scanned it.

"It's official," he said. "The Zaginows will be here tomorrow night."

Senn fretted. "Not much time."

Allan Cole

"It'll do, Senn, dear," Marr soothed. "Otho's pantry is far better stocked than I imagined. We shouldn't have to cheat too much."

Sten hoisted a cleaver and resumed whacking chicken into parts. "Not that I doubt your abilities," he said, "but I don't see how you plan a menu for something like this."

"Well...We want them to be impressed," Marr said. "So the dinner should reflect on your success. However, we want to do business with these people..."

A claw taloned out of the exquisite softness of Marr's fur. It speared a tomato and plunged it into boiling water. "We want them to like us. We don't want them to think we believe we're better than they are, for heaven's sakes."

Marr lifted the tomato from its hot bath - spun it toward the opposite paw. Where another claw whisked away the skin. Snip. Slide. Just like that. Sten's jaw dropped.

On automatic, Marr speared another tomato and repeated the process. And another tomato was peeled. Snip. Slide. Just like that. "Haute cuisine is definitely out, out, out," he said.

Allan Cole

"It wouldn't do," Senn agreed. "Not at all." His wickedly sharp claws were blazing through a stack of yellow onions. Skinning and chopping so deftly, Sten didn't feel the slightest sting in his eyes.

"We've decided on native dishes," Marr said. "Food one might imagine came from an ordinary being's kitchen. But still a little exotic and daring because it is from someplace else."

"Also, it gives us a theme," Senn said, disposing of another onion. "A Flag of All Nations sort of theme. It fits with the jumble of beings that make up the Zaginows."

"We like themes," Marr said.

Sten was only half-listening. He was busy gaping at the Milchens' skills. They were living kitchen machines. Full of all kinds of little tricks.

"Great. Great. Themes and all," Sten said. "But, before you go any further, I have to ask you a question."

"Question away, dear," Marr said, thunking down the last peeled tomato.

"I can't do onions like Senn..." he said, pointing at the furry little whirlwind, chopping up big mounds of the stuff.

Allan Cole

"I'm not built for it. But that trick with the tomatoes...Every time I have to peel tomatoes, I mutilate the suckers. One pound of peel for every ounce of tomato."

"Poor thing," Marr said.

"You only have to dip them in boiling water," Senn said in a small - I really, really, don't think you're stupid - voice.

"And he's the leader of us all," Marr said.

"I did read about it, once," Sten said, weak. "But I never got around to testing it out."

"There, there, dear," Senn said. "Of course you didn't."

The kitchen was filled with the delicious odor of tomatoes, garlic, and onions sizzling in olive oil. Marr tasted, adjusted the paprika, stirred some more, then nodded to Senn, who poured in fresh chicken stock.

Marr clamped a lid on the pot and set it to simmer. "When dinner is served," he told Sten, "you might want to go easy on the soup."

Sten eyed the big pot, "Sure looks like enough to go around to me."

Allan Cole

Senn laughed. "Oh, there's plenty, all right. But this is a special recipe. A guaranteed first-course tension-breaker. For the guests, that is. Not the host. Hosts should beware of this dish."

"You see," Marr elaborated, "After we strain it through a sieve, we're going to stir in some flour and sour cream. Just enough to make it smooth.

"Then...a moment before we serve it...we add vodka. Lots of vodka! And...voila," Senn said. "We give you...Hungarian tomato vodka soup! It's quite potent, too."

"A tongue loosener, huh?" Sten said, dry. "Did you guys ever consider a career as Mantis interrogators?"

"Amateurs," Senn sniffed.

"No challenge at all," Marr said.

****

"After we get the Zaginow delegation nice and soothed," Senn said, "we need to work on their courage." He was dusting chunks of meat with flour, spiked with lots of salt and pepper.

Marr was assembling chopped-up onions, bell peppers, and crushed garlic. "Build them up for a firm commitment," he said.

Senn giggled. "So to speak."

"Don't be dirty," Marr said, putting on a pan doused with olive oil to heat.

"I can't help it," Senn said, the giggles building. "My mind just works that way. Especially when we're cooking mountain oysters."

Sten frowned. He picked up a chunk of the floured meat. Sniffed it. "Don't smell like oysters to me."

"They're calf testicles, dear," Marr explained. "Cut from the little dickens before they're old enough to know what's missing."

"We're going to do them Basque style," Senn said. "The image is so sexy. Muscular brutes with large libidos."

"Makes you want to fry balls all day," Marr said.

Sten looked at the meat he held in his hand. "Sorry, boys," he said. "I hope you know they went for a good cause."

****

Allan Cole

"Now, we need to engage their minds," Marr said.

Sten looked doubtfully at the large heap of bird parts he'd carved up with his cleaver. "Brain power through a clottin' chicken? You've gotta be kidding."

"Stupid animals, yes," Senn said. "But they're so willing. Especially plucked and dressed out. See how patiently they await their marinade?"

"Like the Zaginows?" Sten guessed.

"Excellent, Sten, dear. You're beginning to get the idea," Marr said. "At this point we should have our new friends primed and ready for fresh approaches...Alert them through their taste buds there are endless possibilities once an alliance has been achieved."

"Don't be so stuffy," Senn said. He waved a spice-dusted paw at Sten. "Ignore him. The dish is called jerk chicken, after all," he said.

"I like it...mon," Sten said.

Marr set down the bunch of scallions he was dicing up. "You've heard of it?" He seemed disappointed.

Allan Cole

"From Jamaica, right?" Sten said. "One of the old Earth islands. A place where they smoke rope fibers and drink silly fruit drinks with little parasols on top."

Marr sighed. "Aren't we running out of clean pots, yet?"

"Not a chance," Sten said. "I've only heard of jerk chicken. I'm not moving until I see how this is done."

"In a kitchen," Marr said, "only the chef is permitted to be clever. Pot washers laugh at Chef's cunning jokes. Pot washers peel potatoes. Pot washers are in a constant state of awe at Chef's genius. Pot washers scrape slime from floors. Pot washers duck a lot when sharp objects are thrown at them when they make poor Chef mad. These are only some of the things pot washers do."

Marr sniffed, "What they don't do, is be clever. Pot washers are never, ever clever."

"I promise it'll never happen again," Sten said.

"He really wasn't that clever," Senn said.

"Very well," Marr said. "It can stay. But only if It promises to button Its lip."

"Mmmmmph," Sten grunted, pointed at his zipped lip.

Allan Cole

"Actually, this is a dish even a pot washer could master the first time," Marr said. "It only tastes complex."

He touched a switch under the chopping board and a metal processor revolved up. Pawsful of chopped hot pepper and scallions went into the processor, along with a few bay leaves, some grated ginger, and diced garlic.

"Now the allspice," Marr said. "That's the anchor. You use about five tablespoons for every kilo of meat. Along with one teaspoon each of nutmeg, cinnamon, salt, and pepper."

He dumped the spices into the processor and hit the button. As it whirred, he slowly poured in oil.

"Peanut oil," Marr said. "Just enough for it all to stick together."

In two beats it was done. Sten peered at the goo.

"Another thing pot washers get to do," Marr said, "is smear goo over chicken."

"This is true. Chefs never smear goo," Senn said. "Especially when they're furry."

Sten, the comparatively hairless pot washer, began spreading the marinade over the chicken. Actually, he

Allan Cole

didn't really mind. It smelled wonderful. His mouth watered imagining what it was all going to taste like when Marr and Senn tonged the chicken off the barbecue.

In the corner, he could hear Marr and Senn arguing over the relative merits of pine nuts in Lebanese pilaf. All about him were the warm smells of a dozen dishes bubbling and simmering. He felt relaxed...clear-minded.

On the whole, he thought, he'd much rather be a pot washer than a Hero of the Revolution.

Marr and Senn observed Sten's beaming face as he slathered marinade over chicken.

"Do you think he's ready?" Marr whispered.

"Absolutely," Senn said. "I don't like to pat myself on the back, but I think this is one of the best jobs we've ever done."

"Beings don't realize," Marr said, "that the first - and only - real secret of a dinner party is getting the host prepared first."

"A little kitchen magic," Senn said. "It works every time."

****

Allan Cole

The Zaginow leader forked one more bite from the creamy pastry dish in front of her. She looked at it… as if not believing her body was capable of handling still more. The fork continued its journey and the pastry disappeared into her mouth.

She closed her eyes. Ebony features a portrait of bliss. Tasting. Mmmmm.

Her eyes snapped open to find Sten grinning at her.

"Oh, burp," she said. "Oh, heaven. But, I *just* couldn't eat anymore."

"I think the chefs will forgive you, Ms. Sowazi, if you resign the field of battle," Sten said. "You've certainly given it your best."

He glanced around the banquet room. Marr and Senn had turned the drafty Bhor hall into a wonder of festooned flowers and subtle lights.

The other guests were as dazzled and replete as Sowazi.

For two hours, Marr and Senn had commanded convoy after convoy of deliciousness through the room.

Allan Cole

Whether the dish was meant for a human or an ET, each was greeted and devoured with great enthusiasm.

Beings had their elbows—or equivalent parts—on the tables now. Chatting warmly away with Sten's colleagues as if they were all long-lost friends.

As a capper, Marr and Senn had printed up souvenir menus for each member of the Zaginow delegation.

"We always do it," Marr said. "Beings like to show the folks at home what a good time they had. It's wonderful advertising for us, as well."

"Not 'advertising,' dear," Senn said. "Not in this case, at any rate. Remember, we're revolutionaries now. The military term is 'propaganda'."

"Same thing," Marr sniffed.

"True. But 'propaganda' is much more romantic."

Sten had to admit that the souvenir menus fit the bill perfectly as propaganda.

On the back was a picture of himself, flanked by the master caterers, Marr and Senn.

On the front, Senn got his theme:

"A FEAST FOR ALL BEINGS."

Allan Cole

This was the menu for the humans:

SOUP

Hungarian Tomato Vodka

Miso Saki Shrimp

****

SALAD

Cambodian Raw Fish

Tomato Cucumber Raita

****

APPETIZERS

Basque Mountain Oysters

Russian Blinis and Caviar

Armenian Stuffed Mushrooms

****

ENTREES

Jamaican Jerk Chicken

Moroccan Roast Lamb

Broiled Salmon Steaks

Mesquite Broiled Vegetable Kabob

Allan Cole

SIDE DISHES

Lebanese Rice Pilaf

Rosemary Potatoes

Cuban Black Beans & Rice

****

DESSERT

New York Style Cheesecake

Swedish Pancakes With Lingonberries

****

The items listed on the menus for the ETs were equally impressive.

Sten saw Marr peering from a doorway. He spotted Sten and waved. It was time.

Sten turned to Sowazi. "I think we're being called for coffee and brandy," he said.

She laughed, deep and pleasurable. "Cigars, too?"

"Cigars, too," Sten promised.

"Lead on, Sr. Sten."

As he rose to do her bidding, Sten made a furtive thumbs-up motion to Marr. Everything was going according to plan.

Allan Cole

****

To end this cookbook it is only fitting that we give Kilgour the last word and so we present:

Alex Kilgour's Beef Jerky

…Then Alex allowed himself one of the two indulgences he had promised himself for the mission. He found a grocer's and bought three kilos of inexpensive, thin-sliced lean beef, salt, fresh parsley, and a collection of dried spices. Back at his tenement, he strip-cut the beef, about three centimeters wide. The strips went into a marinade of soy sauce, water, some cheap red wine, some hot sauce, and spices—garlic, a handful of juniper berries, summer savory, pepper. The garlic, berries, and spices were sautéed a bit, and then dumped, hissing hot, into the rest of the marinade. The strips of beef went in to soak for a day.

The strips of beef were drained and laid on the counter. Over them Alex sprinkled salt - at least a pinch per slice. After that, chopped parsley. Then very generous pinches of a potpourri of the spices he'd bought. Thyme. More savory. Sweet basil. Pepper. Garlic pepper. Herb pepper.

Allan Cole

Marjoram. Some cumin, just for the hell of it. He pressed the spices into the meat with the flat of his knife, then flipped the slices over and repeated the seasoning.

The meat went into the tenement's dilapidated oven, set at its absolute lowest, and with a cork holding the oven door open a centimeter or two.

He took a long nap, storing energy for the future. When he awoke just before dusk the slices of beef were dry, twisted, black, thoroughly nasty, and no more than a kilo in total weight.

He admired his jerky. "Ah'm noo th' cook th' Emp, Marr, Senn, or e'en m' wee Sten is. But this'll chew easy, I' th' woods, I' th' rain."

The End

Allan Cole

Sten Cookery:
The Editor Speaks

I originally got to know Allan Cole and Chris Bunch from answering their editor's phone. That was when they'd leave messages saying things like: "Where's our money? We know where your wife works and where your kid goes to school."

They'd throw in some unprintables, which I dutifully took down verbatim. So I guess I was all prepared to take over as their editor on the Sten books eventually.

I never expected to have an AK-47 shoved in my hands and a camera flashed in my face...but hey, that's what we editors will do for authors we like!

Now all eight Sten books are on my shelves, and the photo is on my refrigerator...though I haven't yet tried one of the recipes in the books...

Shelly Shapiro, Executive Editor, Del Rey Books

Allan Cole

About The Sten Series

Hailed as a "landmark science fiction series" the Sten novels have thrilled millions of readers all over the world.

Set three thousand years in the future, the eight Sten novels tell the tale of a tough, street-wise orphan who escapes his fate as factory planet "delinq" to become the strong right-hand of the most powerful man in the Universe – a man hailed by his billons of subjects as "The Eternal Emperor."

THE HERO

Sten is the ultimate survivor. He's lightning quick, mean streets cunning and blessed with the twin gifts of hungry intelligence and hard-won common sense. Born on a factory planet where life has less value than the lowliest

Allan Cole

machine, Sten rebels against The Company that enslaved, then killed his parents. He finds a new family of sorts - and the means for revenge - in the ranks of the Emperor's Imperial Forces.

A series of crucial missions brings him to the attention of the Eternal Emperor himself. Sten's talents and unshakable loyalty are tested in crisis after crisis, brutal warfare and assassination.

Besides his "black ops" skills, Sten is armed with a weapon of last resort – he carries a small knife made of an undetectable substance in a flesh and muscle "sheath" in his arm. With a blade edge only one molecule thick, the knife can cut through any substance like butter.

Sten rises swiftly until he becomes a confidante and advisor to the Emperor. Through all this Sten never forgets his lowly origins. Self-depreciating humor, friendship and luck in love shield him from Fame's blinding light. If anything his empathy and sense of responsibility for the common folk of the Empire grow with each new honor and badge of rank.

Allan Cole

Finally he is asked to make the supreme sacrifice - risking even those he loves - to stand up for the citizens of the Empire. Then, when he succeeds, he turns his back on the greatest honor of all.

STEN'S WORLD

Picture the greatest Empire history has known. Its boundaries are the Universe itself, containing more stars, planets and sentient life than could be calculated by the swiftest 21st Century computer. This is a space kingdom where humans live side-by-side with countless alien forms. In fact the word alien itself is offensive and all species are merely called "beings." The planetary systems range from the sophistication of Prime World where the elite gather - to the rough and ready mining and frontier worlds at the Empire's edges.

Ruling over all this is:

THE ETERNAL EMPEROR

As his title implies, the Eternal Emperor is a human who has mastered death through the use of secret cloning

Allan Cole

techniques and mind transfer. When he's in his cups, he sometimes boasts that although he's been the target of hundreds of assassination, only three were successful.

The Emperor is the ultimate capitalist and when Sten steps onto the stage he has reigned for three thousand years. The source of the Eternal Emperor's power is a mysterious fuel - called Anti-Matter Two (AM2). It drives the star ships that link the Empire and provides the energy for all industry, agriculture and commerce. He alone controls its supply and price. And he alone knows where AM2 is to be found.

The Emperor is no tyrant. He prefers wit to force, negotiation to confrontation. But if all else fails he has enormous military resources to back up his will. His past is a rigorously guarded secret and his future is permanently entwined with the Empire he created.

Despite his vast power the Emperor greatly misses the familiar things of his 21st Century youth. On a bad day he would trade it all in for a good bottle of single malt scotch or the sweet sound of an old, hand-crafted violin. He spends his spare time in his antique-cluttered royal suites,

Allan Cole

restoring or re-constructing nostalgic objects from his salad days.

The Emperor, who has the looks of a handsome, 35-year-old, is also a consummate cook and spends hours in his Prime World kitchens recreating the recipes of ancient Earth, while hatching elaborate plans to confound his many enemies.

The Eternal Emperor sees a bit of his long ago self in Sten. After all, as he occasionally implies, his roots are as common as Sten's. If their relationship was not by necessity that of ruler and subject they might even have become friends.

Sten admires the Emperor. Perhaps, in a way, he even considers him a father figure. And he has sworn absolute loyalty to the Empire. In the end, however, he will realize that his loyalty is to the idea not the man.

OTHER CHARACTERS

Sten's world is filled with bizarre and wonderful characters. Among the more important are:

Allan Cole

ALEX KILGOUR: Sten's sidekick and confidant. An incredibly strong heavy-worlder of Scots descent, Kilgour's passion is shaggy-dog stories. All of which are so awful that his mission mates can hardly wait for the bad guys to kick in the door and interrupt him.

IAN MAHONEY: Sten's mentor. A top military man, Mahoney excels at both cloak-and-dagger and more conventional warfare, and prefers to lead from the front. He is totally loyal to Emperor.

DOC: A furry alien with the psionic talent to make people like him. It helps that humans think he's a cute, cuddly teddy-bear. Carnivorous little Doc would just love to tear their throats out for that.

IDA: The brilliant Gypsy operative (and hotrod pilot) whose hobby is making huge amounts on the stock market. She could easily retire, but she loves the challenges and danger of black operations work. Fat, mustached and foul-mouthed, she delights in harassing authority.

Allan Cole

And there are many more, including the various beautiful and multi-talented women Sten squires during his adventures. Ranging from a tough Prime World detective, to the princess of a barbaric race of space pirates.

(For links To All Versions And Formats Of Sten go to http://tinyurl.com/3go7w5n)

Allan Cole

About The Authors

International bestselling authors and screenwriters Allan Cole and the late Chris Bunch were collaborators for nearly twenty years. Together and separately they published over forty novels and sold more than 150 screenplays. Their most noteworthy science fiction collaboration produced the eight-book Sten series, hailed as "landmark science fiction" by Publishers Weekly, among others. For details about Allan's life and work, see his homepage at http://www.acole.com. For information about Chris, see his Wikipedia entry at http://www.en.wikipedia.org/wiki/Chris_Bunch. Both authors are also featured in the International Movie Data Base - http://www.IMDB.com . To buy the Sten series, or peruse other books by Bunch & Cole, stop by Allan's Bookstore: http://tinyurl.com/l9mpr5 And to read about their hilarious years working the gilded trenches of Tinsel Town, visit Allan's popular blog, My Hollywood MisAdventures at: http://allan-cole.blogspot.com/

·

www.ingramcontent.com/pod-product-compliance
Lightning Source LLC
Chambersburg PA
CBHW070631130626

46555CB00006B/2523